If you have a home computer with Internet access you may:
- request an item to be placed on hold.
- renew an item that is not overdue or on hold.
- view titles and due dates checked out on your card.
- view and/or pay your outstanding fines online (over $5).

To view your patron record from your home computer click on Patchogue-Medford Library's homepage: www.pmlib.org

PiCNiC at CaMP SHaLOM

To Debbie Locke, a wonderful friend, in times
of need and joy, to me and many others. — J.J.

For my mom, with much love. — D.M

KAR-BEN Publishing, Inc.
A division of Lerner Publishing Group
241 First Avenue North
Minneapolis, MN 55401 U.S.A.
800-4KARBEN

Website address: www.karben.com

Library of Congress Cataloging-in-Publication Data

Jules, Jacqueline, 1956-
    Picnic at Camp Shalom / by Jacqueline Jules ; illustrated by Deborah Melmon.
      p.   cm.
    Summary: At summer camp, Carlie and Sara quickly bond over a love of singing
and other shared interests, but Sara mistakes Carlie excitement over her surname as
teasing, not knowing that it gives them something else in common.
    ISBN 978-0-7613-6661-4 (lib. bdg. : alk. paper) [1. Friendship—Fiction.
2. Camps—Fiction. 3. Jews—Fiction. 4. Names, Personal—Fiction.] I. Melmon, Deborah,
ill. II. Title.
PZ7.J92947Pic 2011
[E]—dc22

2010027797

Manufactured in the United States of America
1 – DP – 12/31/10

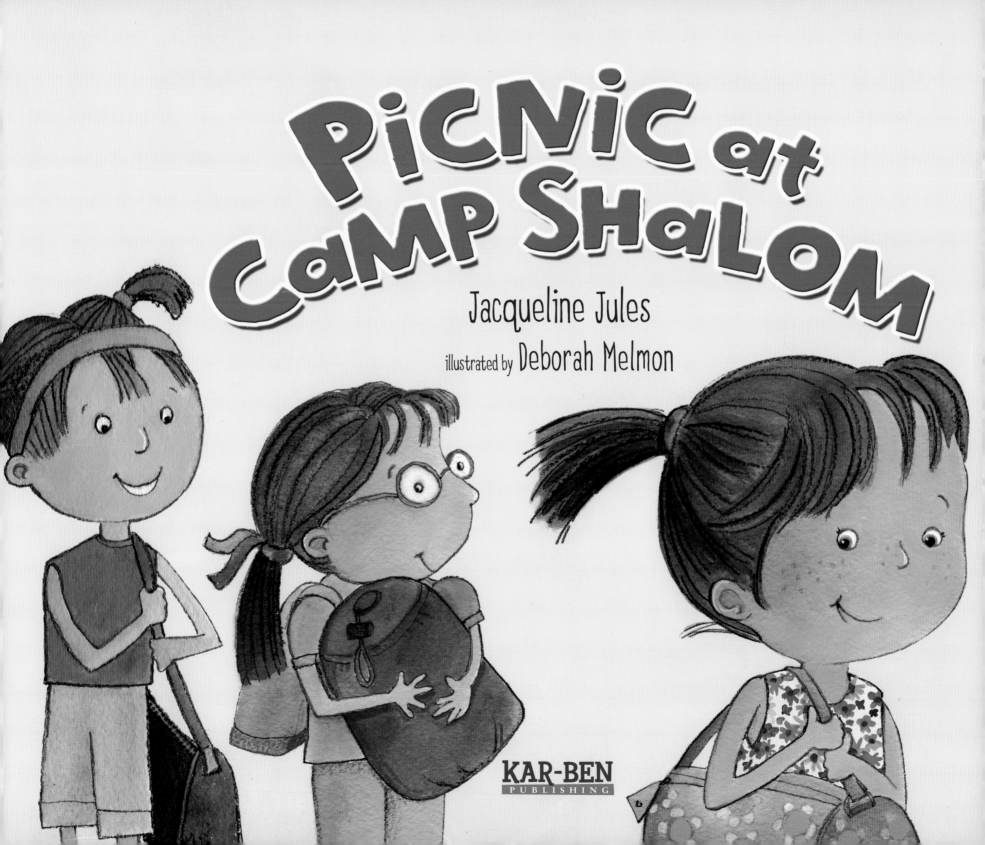

PicNiC at CaMP ShaLOM

Jacqueline Jules

illustrated by Deborah Melmon

KAR-BEN
PUBLISHING

Someone giggled behind me as I waited in line for the swim test.
I turned around and saw a girl with red, curly hair.

She was wearing a blue bathing suit with silver stars.
It was exactly like mine.

"Twins!" she said, smiling.

"Aren't you in my cabin?" I asked. I remembered seeing a
girl with red hair rush in, just as we were leaving for the lake.

"Yes, I came in late. My name is Sara."

"I'm Carly."

We talked some more while we waited our turn.

After the swim test, our counselor Jenny called everyone together for a scavenger hunt. Sara chose me as her partner, and we ran all over camp hunting for "Welcome to Camp Shalom" flags. We found the most and won a prize.

"Good teamwork!" Jenny said, giving us each a beaded necklace.

Welcome
to
Camp
Shalom

"Lights out" for our cabin was at 9 o'clock, but Sara and I whispered for an extra hour. We discovered that both of us love music. Sara told me she sang with the band at her sister's Bat Mitzvah party. I told her about my solo at my school's choral concert.

The next day just after swimming, Jenny stood at the cabin door waving an envelope. "Mail call!" she announced. "Sara wins the prize for the first letter from home."

"She's inside changing. I'll give it to her," I said, taking the letter and reading the name on the envelope.

"FRANKFURTER!" I shouted when Sara came out. "Your last name is FRANKFURTER! LIKE THE HOTDOG!" I opened my arms to give her a hug.

Sara grabbed her letter. "My name's not funny," she said in a cold voice.

Before I could explain, she ran down the path to the dining hall.

"What happened?" Jenny asked, when she saw me eating alone.
"Did you and Sara have a fight?"

As I told Jenny about my mistake, tears spilled onto my sandwich.
"Sara thinks I made fun of her name. But it's exactly the opposite!"

At home, everybody had short, plain names like "Jones" or "Walker." Finding a friend named Frankfurter was like finding a twin.

"You were just excited," Jenny said. "Sara will understand."

But for the rest of the day, Sara avoided me. At the lake, she shared a paddleboat with someone else.

When we played volleyball, she made
sure to be on the opposite side.

In the Crafts Barn, she worked at
the table farthest away from me.

I couldn't get anywhere near her until we went to the Music House. She sat down in the front row, and I grabbed the seat beside her. Sara put her finger on her lips.

"Shhh! Jenny's talking," she said.

"Tomorrow is Shabbat," Jenny said, passing out music sheets. "Our bunk will lead the singing after dinner."

The first song she taught us was about friendship. I sang as loudly as I could, hoping Sara would feel a message from me.

"That sounds beautiful!" Jenny clapped. "But we can make it more interesting. Let's start this song off as a duet, and then have everybody else join in."

A duet! That meant two people would be picked to sing together. I closed my eyes, wishing.

"Sara and Carly." Jenny pointed at us. "Come up here and give it a try."

Sara and I stood side by side, practicing the song. She opened her mouth wide, but the rest of her body was stiff, like a wall. And when we were done, she ran out of the room.

"Give Sara some space," Jenny said. "She'll listen once she cools off."

The next night, everyone put on white clothes for Shabbat. The light from the candles sparkled over our faces as we sang the blessings. Our voices echoed in the big room.

We sat down to matzah ball soup, challah, and roasted chicken. "Weekends at camp are great," Jenny said, "from Shabbat dinner to the Sunday picnic."

After we ate, it was time to sing. Jenny gave me an extra job as we got up from the table. "Introduce yourself and Sara before the song," she whispered.

"Finally!" I thought. "A way to make Sara listen to me!"

"Shabbat Shalom!" I began. The room got so quiet I thought I could hear the candles flicker. "My name is Carly Hamburger."

"HAMBURGER? LIKE CHOPPED MEAT?" Sara whispered.

I nodded with a big smile. Sara took my hand. Every note we sang together sounded perfect to me.

Afterwards, on the way back to the cabin, Sara told me about a girl at school who makes hot dog jokes about her name.

"A boy at my school teases me with hamburger and French fry jokes," I told her.

The darkness was a tent, giving us a quiet place to share our secrets.

"Hamburger and Frankfurter." I giggled. "Two girls with the same problem at school."

"But not at camp," Sara laughed. "Here we're just what you need for the Sunday picnic."

Jacqueline Jules is an award-winning author and poet. Her children's books include *Sarah Laughs* and *Benjamin and the Silver Goblet* (Sydney Taylor Honor Award winners), *The Hardest Word* and *The Princess and the Ziz*. She has two grown sons and lives in Northern Virginia with her husband.

Deborah Melmon has illustrated greeting cards, cookbooks, and children's books; she also has created environmental art for the California Science Museum. She first realized she was going to be an artist when a papier-mâché lion she created in seventh-grade art class grew so large that it had to be driven home in the trunk of her parents' Oldsmobile with the lid up!